THE ZACK FILES

Great-Grandpa's in the Litter Box

For Judith, and for the real Zack,
with love—D.G.

THE ZACK FILES™

Great-Grandpa's in the Litter Box

By Dan Greenburg

Illustrated by Jack E. Davis

GROSSET & DUNLAP • NEW YORK

I'd like to thank my editors,
Jane O'Connor and Judy Donnelly,
who make the process of writing and revising
so much fun, and without whom
these books would not exist.

I also want to thank
Jennifer Dussling and Laura Driscoll
for their terrific ideas.

Text copyright © 1996 by Dan Greenburg. Illustrations copyright © 1996 by Jack E.
Davis. All rights reserved. Published by Grosset & Dunlap, Inc., a member of Penguin
Putnam Books for Young Readers, New York. THE ZACK FILES is a trademark of The
Putnam & Grosset Group. GROSSET & DUNLAP is a trademark of Grosset & Dunlap,
Inc. Published simultaneously in Canada. Printed in the U.S.A.

Library of Congress Cataloging-in-Publication Data

Greenburg, Dan.
   Great-Grandpa's in the litter box / by Dan Greenburg ; illustrated by Jack E. Davis.
      p.   cm. – (The Zack files)
   Summary: Zack takes home from the local animal shelter a scruffy tomcat who not
only talks but claims to be the reincarnation of Zack's Great-Grandpa Julius.
   [1. Cats–Fiction. 2. Reincarnation–Fiction. 3. Great-grandfathers–Fiction.
4. Supernatural–Fiction.]   I. Davis, Jack E., ill. II. Title. III. Series: Greenburg, Dan.
Zack files.
PZ7.G8278Gr 1996
[Fic]–dc20   96-7117
                                                                                                     CIP
                                                                                                     AC

ISBN   0-448-41260-8   I J

Chapter

1

My name is Zack. I'm ten years old and I guess you could say I've been interested in weird stuff all my life. Stuff like haunted houses, UFOs, and storms where it rains frogs. So when something weird happened to me, I was probably more open-minded than somebody else who wasn't interested in weird stuff all their life.

I was in the animal shelter near our home in New York City. After years of begging my dad for a cat, he finally broke down and said yes. I could get a kitten. So here I was.

I passed a cage with an old gray tomcat inside it. His fur was matted with dirt. He'd lost half the whiskers on the left side of his face, which made him look a little lopsided. And the tip had been chewed off of one of his ears.

"Sssst! Young man!" Someone was calling me. The voice sounded raspy and strange. "Hello, little boy! Over here!"

I turned around, looking to see who it was. But there was nobody in sight.

I went on to a cage where a little tuxedo kitten with a black body and white paws was taking a nap. He sure was cute. I stopped to take a closer look at him. Of course, it probably wasn't the best time for me to adopt a kitten. In a couple of days my dad and I were flying to Chicago to spend Thanksgiving with my Grandma Leah. But our neighbor had agreed to cat-sit. And I wasn't taking any chances of my dad changing his mind.

I'd almost decided on that cute little tuxedo kitten when I heard the voice again:

"Hey, kid," said the voice. "I am *speaking* to you."

"Where are you?" I asked.

"Right here, dummy," said the voice. "In the cage in back of you."

I turned around. That scruffy old gray tomcat was staring quite crossly at me.

"You'll pardon me for hollering," said the cat. "But I was afraid you were about to make a terrible mistake and choose somebody else."

"You can *talk*!" I said, hardly able to believe my ears.

I moved closer to his cage. I wanted to see if his cat lips moved when he talked. Maybe this was just a trick—somebody doing ventriloquism. I mean I told you I like weird stuff, but this was really far out, even for me. "A talking cat?" I said.

"Yeah, a talking cat, how about that," said the cat sarcastically.

His cat lips were moving! This was no trick!

"But look at you—a talking boy," he said. "Listen, we don't have much time. You've got to get me out of here."

"What do you mean?"

"I mean I can't stand it in here a minute longer," he said. "The meowing and the

smell are driving me right up the wall. Tell them you're adopting me."

"Uh, I don't mean to hurt your feelings," I said. "But I've already decided on this little tuxedo kitten here." Like I said before, I'm pretty open-minded. I had nothing against talking cats. I just wasn't sure I wanted to live with one. Especially with one as bossy as this one seemed.

"The tuxedo kitten?" he said. "Poor choice."

"What do you mean?"

"He has fleas and worms. Plus he never got the hang of using a litter box."

The tomcat gave me a long look. He could see I wasn't buying it.

"OK," the cat went on. "I didn't want to have to use this. But here goes: If you don't adopt me, they're going to put me to sleep.

And I don't mean tuck me in bed in my jammies either. I mean kill me. You really want that on your conscience, kid?"

"Listen, they don't put cats to sleep here," I said. "That is a well-known fact." This cat was not only bossy, he also seemed to have problems with the truth.

"OK, I admit they haven't lately," he said. "But that could change any day."

I looked at him and shook my head.

"OK, OK," he said. "How's about this: What if I told you I know your name?"

"What's my name?"

"Zack."

"How—how did you know that?" I asked. I had to admit I was pretty impressed. Not that many people know my name, and even fewer cats.

"You're impressed, huh?" said the big

gray tomcat. "What if I told you I'm a member of your family, Zack? Do you think you'd still prefer the little tuxedo?"

"A member of my *family*?" I said. "How could that be? You're a cat."

"Hey, you never heard of reincarnation? Somebody dies and comes back as somebody else?"

"So?" I said. Sure, I'd heard of reincarnation. In fact, I'd read about several cases in India of kids who claimed to have lived before. They knew facts about certain places they'd never been, things they couldn't possibly have known if they were ordinary kids. Still, they were kids, not cats. "So what?"

"So," said the gray tomcat, "I happen to be your wonderful dead Great-Grandfather Julius."

Chapter 2

One minute I'm about to go home with a cute little black-and-white kitten, the next a big gray tomcat tells me he's my dead great-grandfather. I didn't know what to do. I took another look at the kitten. He was licking his front paw in an adorable way. The tomcat saw I was still leaning toward the kitten.

"What? You don't think I'm cute?" he asked. Then he posed in what he must have thought was a cute pose.

"You're...*kind* of cute, sir," I said. "It's just that..."

"Cute, shmute," he said. "You can't tell me you're going to walk out of here with a flea-bitten stranger who hasn't been properly toilet-trained and leave your beloved great-grandfather rotting in a stinking little cage? Family is family, Zack."

I looked at the tomcat, then at the kitten, then at the tomcat. *Family is family.* Funny, that's something Grandma Leah always says. That did it.

"I guess you're right, sir," I said. "I guess family is family."

"Now you're talking sense, kid," said the cat. "And, please, call me Great-Grandpa Julius."

Chapter 3

When I arrived home, huffing and puffing, carrying my cardboard cat carrier, my dad met me at the door. Since my parents split up, I live part of the time with my dad and part with my mom.

"So," he said, smiling, "it looks like you've finally gotten yourself a kitty."

"Yeah," I said, and put the cat carrier down. I was exhausted. With Great-Grandpa Julius inside it, it must have weighed close to thirty pounds.

"Can I see the little guy?" asked my dad.

"Sure, Dad," I said. "But first I have to tell you a couple of things."

"OK, what?"

"Well, number one, I didn't get a kitten. I got a slightly older cat."

"Why, Zack," said my dad, "I think that's a wonderful thing to do, giving an older cat a home. I'm very proud of you, son."

"Uh-huh. And number two, he's not an ordinary cat, Dad. He's...well, for one thing, he talks."

"He talks," said my dad.

"Yeah, he talks."

My dad smiled, deciding to go along with my little joke.

"I see. Well, what does he say?"

"He says he's Great-Grandpa Julius."

"I didn't even think you remembered having a Great-Grandpa Julius," he said, chuckling.

What I remembered was hearing Grandma Leah go on about her father, Julius, who was so nice he was practically a saint. Then she'd always add how Julius was the complete opposite of Great-Grandpa Maurice, her husband's father. Maurice was the black sheep of the family.

So far, Julius didn't seem that saintly to me. I opened the cat carrier. Great-Grandpa Julius and my dad took a good long look at each other.

"Well, he's certainly...big," said my dad. "Hello, Great-Grandpa Julius. Remember me? Dan? You always used to say I was your favorite grandchild. Can you say hello?"

Great-Grandpa Julius seemed about to say something. Then he scratched behind his ear with his hind leg instead.

"He's not very talkative," said my dad.

"You should have heard him at the animal shelter," I said.

My dad chuckled and walked off, shaking his head.

"How come you didn't talk to my dad?" I asked.

"I talk when I want to," said the cat, "not when other people want me to. Hey, Zack, you got anything to eat around here? I'm so hungry I could eat rodents."

I had the free can of cat food they gave me at the animal shelter. I put it into a bowl on the floor. Great-Grandpa Julius sniffed it and wrinkled up his nose.

"Feh!" he said. "What *is* that stuff?"

"Beef by-products in gravy," I replied.

"You got maybe a little herring with sour cream?"

I told him we didn't have anything like that. He did not take this at all well.

"Let's put it this way, kid," said Great-Grandpa Julius. "Either get me some herring with sour cream pronto, or I'm going to take a leak on your sofa."

"You're not serious about this," I said.

"Try me," he said.

If you ask me, Great-Grandpa Julius was a lot crankier than I'd heard. But I was trying to be understanding. I guess dying and getting reincarnated as a cat could spoil a person's mood.

Chapter 4

Luckily, the deli on the corner sold herring with sour cream. I brought it back to Great-Grandpa Julius.

"Now you're talking," he said when he saw it. He gobbled it up. "Not bad. Not bad at all. But tomorrow, Zack, be sure the deli man doesn't skimp on the sour cream."

Boy, this cat was pushy!

"Listen, I can't buy you herring and sour cream every day," I said. "I only get three dollars a week allowance. And I won't be able to buy it for you over Thanksgiving weekend—I won't even be here. I'm going to Chicago. To visit Grandma Leah."

"We're going to visit Leah?" he asked delightedly.

"*I* am," I said. "You're staying here with a neighbor."

"You'd go to Chicago and you wouldn't take me to see my own daughter? If Leah heard I was reincarnated and didn't come to see her, she'd be crushed."

"Well," I said, "let me ask my dad."

⌇

"Zack," said my dad, "I'm willing to go along with a joke. But we both know cats can't talk. Although I must admit I'm tempted to bring him to Chicago, just to see the expression on Grandma Leah's face when you tell her that cat is her father."

"Dad, I'd really like to take him to Chicago. I think it would mean a lot to him."

"I'll tell you what," said my dad. "If you can get him to talk to me, you can take him to Chicago."

I went back to my room, where Great-Grandpa Julius was pawing through my collection of baseball cards.

"You have any cards with Lou Gehrig, Ty Cobb, or Rogers Hornsby on them?" he asked.

"No, I'm afraid not."

"Gehrig and Hornsby were nice fellas. Cobb not so nice."

"That's what I hear."

"But all three signed my baseball."

"You're saying you actually met Lou Gehrig, Ty Cobb, and Rogers Hornsby?" I said. The tomcat nodded. "What happened to the ball they signed?"

"I have it."

"Where?"

"In a safe place, don't worry about it. So did your dad say I could come to Chicago?"

"He said on one condition."

"What's that?"

"You have to talk to him. I don't think he believes you can talk."

"That's all I have to do, talk to him?"

"That's all."

"OK, let's do it."

I followed Great-Grandpa Julius, who padded into the living room, where my dad was reading the newspaper.

"Dad," I said, "Great-Grandpa Julius has something to say to you."

"Really?" said my dad. He put down his

paper and turned toward the cat, with a big smile on his face. "All right," he said. "Tell me. What was the hardest part about changing from a person into a cat?"

Great-Grandpa Julius looked at my dad a moment without speaking. Then he cocked his head, opened his mouth, and said, "For me, I guess the hardest part was finding out there wasn't a door you could lock behind you on the litter box. Is that good enough for a trip to Chicago?"

My dad's eyes looked like they were going to pop right out of his head.

"Sounds good enough to me," I said. "How about you, Dad?"

Chapter 5

Once my dad found out my cat was Great-Grandpa Julius, he kept asking him questions about what it was like being dead. Dad never let up for the two days before we left for Chicago, and all during the long ride to the airport.

"Some people who died and were brought back to life again claim they went through what looked like a very long tunnel with very bright light at the other end," said my dad. "And all their dead relatives met them on the other side. Did that happen to you?"

"I do remember going through a long tunnel and coming out to bright light on the other side," said Great-Grandpa Julius.

"You do?" said my dad excitedly.

"Yes," said Great-Grandpa Julius. "It happened to be the Midtown Tunnel. And the bright light on the other side was Queens. That's where they buried me. Tell me something. Would you happen to have a cigar on you? It's been years since I've smoked a really good cigar."

"You should stop smoking cigars," I said. "They're bad for you."

"I guess you're right," said Great-Grandpa Julius. "But some things you just don't stop craving, even after you're dead."

"How long have you been a cat?" asked my dad.

"I don't have a driver's license on me," said Great-Grandpa Julius. "How old do I look?"

"About twelve or thirteen," I said.

"That feels about right," he said. "Of course, I didn't come back as a cat right away."

"You didn't?"

"Oh no. First I was a caterpillar."

"A caterpillar?" I said. "What was that like?"

"Extremely boring. Mostly it was about eating leaves. I ate leaves and tried to pretend they were herring with sour cream. Say, you wouldn't by any chance happen to have a little schnapps on you?"

"What's schnapps?" I asked.

"Liquor," said my dad. "No, I'm sorry, I don't carry schnapps on me."

We arrived at the airport. Dad paid the cab driver. I tried to put Great-Grandpa Julius back into his cat carrier.

"Hey, c'mon," he cried. "Don't make me travel in a suitcase again. I'm a dignified old geezer, for Pete's sake."

"In a past life you were a dignified old geezer," I said. "In *this* life you're a stray cat. And cats travel in cat carriers."

Julius sighed and got into his carrier.

Once we got on the plane, Dad started in again with his questions.

"So, Julius," said Dad, "after you were a caterpillar, did you become a butterfly?"

"No, a moth," said the voice inside the cat carrier. "Mostly that was about eating sweaters."

"You ate sweaters?" I said. "Ugh!"

"Don't knock it till you've tried it," said Great-Grandpa Julius. "I remember one fine cashmere turtleneck. It was almost as tasty as a corned beef on rye. Then one night I happened to fly a little too close to a torch outside a Polynesian restaurant and—pffft!"

"Another tunnel?"

"No, no, moths don't get tunnels. Only humans get tunnels. After that I became a mouse."

"And that was all about eating cheese, I suppose," said my dad.

"No, about eating wood. Don't ask."

"Wait a minute," I said. "First you were a caterpillar, then you were a moth, then a mouse. How did you have time to be all those things?"

"We're not talking about a lot of time here," said Great-Grandpa Julius. "You could die, do a stretch as a caterpillar, then a moth, then a mouse, and you could still be back by a week from Thursday. But time didn't matter to me. I was dead. I had quite a lot of leisure time on my hands."

"Excuse me," said the flight attendant as she passed our row. "In preparation for takeoff, please make sure your seat belts are securely fastened and that your seat backs and tray tables are in the upright and locked position."

"Hey, cookie," said Great-Grandpa Julius, "what are you doing after the flight?"

The flight attendant thought my dad said that, because she gave him a dirty look.

Then we buckled up. Next stop—Chicago!

Chapter 6

"Before we see her, I just want to ask you one thing," said my dad in the elevator of the building on Lake Shore Drive where Grandma Leah lives.

"What's that?" I asked.

"Grandma Leah is in her eighties. Do you really think it's safe to tell a woman in her eighties that her dead father is now a cat?"

"Grandma Leah is a very peppy, open-minded person," I replied. "I'm sure she'll take the news OK."

The elevator doors opened on the seventh floor and we walked down the hall to Grandma Leah's apartment, my dad carrying our luggage and me carrying the carrier with Great-Grandpa Julius in it.

Grandma Leah was so happy to see us. She kept hugging and kissing us all over the place. When we were all settled in her apartment she noticed the cat carrier for the first time.

"Don't tell me you brought an animal all the way to Chicago?" she said.

"Not just any animal, Grandma," I said. "A very special animal."

"Special in what way?" asked Grandma Leah.

"Special in the way that he is not only a cat, he is also a member of our family," I said.

"In other words, you love him so much you feel he's a member of our family?" asked Grandma Leah.

I looked at my dad and then back at Grandma Leah.

"No," I said, "I mean he really is a member of our family."

And with that I opened up the cat carrier. Grandma Leah and Great-Grandpa Julius took their first look at each other.

"Grandma Leah," I said, "I believe this is your father, Great-Grandpa Julius."

Grandma Leah stared at the cat in silence for a moment and then shook her head.

"No," she said. "I don't believe it is. My father was taller."

"Leah dear," said Great-Grandpa Julius, "it's so wonderful to see you again. How have you been all these years, my darling?"

"It's talking to me," said Grandma Leah in a very strange voice. "A cat is talking to me in the English language."

"He is," I said.

"Leah dear," said Great-Grandpa Julius, "I may be a cat, but I'm also your father."

"It's still talking to me," said Grandma Leah. "Am I right about this, that the cat is still talking to me?"

"You're right," I said.

"Tell the cat I said it's not my father," she said.

"Why don't you tell him yourself?" I suggested.

"I don't talk to cats," said Grandma Leah in the same strange voice.

"Grandma Leah says you're not her father," I said.

"I *heard* her, I *heard* her," said Great-Grandpa Julius. "What am I, deaf?" Then the cat softened his voice. "Leah dear, don't you remember me? It's Daddy!"

"Tell the cat I said that we never called my father by the name of Daddy," said Grandma Leah. "Ask it what we called my real father."

"She says what name did she call you?" I asked.

"I heard her, I heard her." Great-Grandpa Julius's voice was rising. "You don't have to repeat everything she says."

"Well then, what name did she call you?"

"It wasn't Daddy," said Great-Grandpa Julius.

"We've already heard her say it wasn't Daddy," said my dad.

"Of course it wasn't Daddy," said Great-Grandpa Julius. "Because it was... Father."

Grandma Leah shook her head.

"Tell the cat it wasn't Father," said Grandma Leah.

"She says it wasn't—"

"*Don't repeat it!*" snapped Great-Grandpa Julius angrily. Then he quickly recovered his composure. "It wasn't Father. Of course it wasn't Father," he said. "Father was what I called myself. What you called me was...Papa."

"Tell the cat it wasn't Papa," said Grandma Leah.

"Oh boy," said Great-Grandpa Julius.

"Could I ever use a good cigar or a glass of schnapps right about now. Leah dear, I'm over a hundred years old. I've been a cater-pillar, a moth, a mouse. I've died many times, so my memory isn't quite what it used to be. Could you please give me a break here and tell me what you used to call me?"

"Go on, Grandma Leah," I said. "Tell him what you used to call him."

"I didn't call the *cat* anything," she said. "I called my *father*—my real father, my human father—Poppy."

"Poppy, shmoppy," said Great-Grandpa Julius. He waved his paw dismissively. "How far is Poppy from Papa?"

"Wait a minute," said Grandma Leah. "I just realized something."

"What's that?" I said.

"Did the cat say it wanted a good cigar or a glass of schnapps?"

"That's what he said," I said.

"My father, Julius, never smoked cigars. And he never drank schnapps. You know who smoked cigars and drank schnapps?"

"Who?" I said.

"Who?" said my dad.

"The black sheep of the family, that's who. Your cat is a liar, Zack. He's not my father, Julius, at all. He's your grandpa's no-good father. He's Great-Grandpa Maurice!"

Chapter 7

"Is what Grandma Leah says true?" I demanded of the large gray tomcat. "Are you my grandpa's no-good father, Maurice?"

"Now, hold your horses, sonny, hold your horses," he said. "First of all, where does she get off calling me a no-good?"

"Where do I get off?" said Grandma Leah angrily. "I'll tell you where I get off. You took thirty thousand dollars of my father's money to work on your crazy inventions. Then you left town. Disappeared. We never heard a word from you again."

We all turned to the cat.

"What inventions?" I asked.

"I'll tell you what inventions," said Grandma Leah. "A hairpiece for bald eagles was one."

"Who would ever buy a hairpiece for bald eagles?" I asked the cat.

"Well, that was a problem," said the cat.

"Then there was the dog whistle," Grandma Leah went on. "Only dogs were supposed to be able to hear it."

"That sounds better," I said.

"Except for one little thing," she said. The cat looked embarrassed. "Dogs could not hear it either. You blew it and all the mice in the neighborhood came running."

"Did you invent anything that worked?" I asked.

"Yes!" said the cat. "A sweater for dachshunds in the shape of a hot dog bun. Very cute, if I do say so myself. At first it didn't sell. I thought I'd lost all of Julius's money, so I beat it out of town. But you know what? After a while that sweater started selling like crazy. Everybody who owned a dachshund had to have one. I made back the whole thirty thousand. I had it sent directly to a secret bank account in Chicago."

"A secret bank account?" I said.

"In the Morton F. Acropolis Savings and Loan Association of Chicago," said the cat. "I was coming to Chicago to pay Julius back when I got hit by a Greyhound bus."

We all stared at the cat.

"Great-Grandpa Maurice," I said gently. "You've told us many things that weren't true. How do we know what you're telling us now is the truth?"

"First thing tomorrow morning," he said, "take me to the Morton F. Acropolis Savings and Loan Association of Chicago. Then you'll find out."

Chapter 8

And so the next morning, right after breakfast, my dad, my Grandma Leah, my Great-Grandpa Maurice, and I all got into a cab and went to the Morton F. Acropolis Savings and Loan Association of Chicago.

At first the bank officer we spoke with told us she couldn't find any secret bank account bearing the number Maurice had given us.

"Tell her to look harder," said Maurice from inside the cat carrier.

The bank officer looked startled.

"Please look harder, ma'am," I said.

And so the bank officer looked harder.

"You'd better be telling us the truth about this," I said to the cat carrier.

"Don't be so mistrustful," said the voice from inside the cat carrier.

The bank officer returned.

"I did find something," she said. "An account was opened a great many years ago. I don't know if it's the right one. But it does bear the same number you gave me."

"What's the name on the account?" I asked.

"That, of course, would be a secret," said the bank officer.

"What if I told you the first name?" I said. "Would you just nod your head if I'm right?"

"What name are you thinking of?" she asked.

"Maurice," I said.

The bank officer nodded.

"I'm right!" I said. Great-Grandpa Maurice was telling the truth! "Now how do we get the money?"

"Well, the individual whose name is on the account would have to sign for it," she said.

We all looked at each other.

"What if he couldn't do that?" asked my dad.

"Why couldn't he do that?" said the bank officer.

"What if he were...What if something had happened to him?" I said.

"Such as what?" said the bank officer.

"Such as, oh, I don't know, such as he

turned into a cat," I said.

"Such as he *died*," said my dad quickly.

"Well, if the account holder is deceased," said the bank officer, "then the money would go into probate. Probate is a very long, very complicated legal process. It takes years to sort out."

"What does deceased mean?" I whispered.

"Dead," said the voice inside the cat carrier.

"What if he turned into a cat?" I asked.

"Excuse me?" said the bank officer.

My dad looked at me and shook his head.

"Do you believe in reincarnation?" I asked the bank officer.

"No," she said.

We all looked at each other. We didn't

have any idea what to do next.

"Hey," said the voice in the cat carrier, "can I talk to her?"

"Is there somebody inside that animal carrier?" asked the bank officer, alarmed.

"Hey, let me out of here!" said the voice.

I looked at my dad. He shrugged. I opened the cat carrier. Great-Grandpa Maurice hopped out onto the counter.

"Uh, I'm afraid pets aren't allowed inside the bank," said the bank officer, "The regulations specifically forbid— "

"Oh, pipe down a minute, sis," said Great-Grandpa Maurice. "And maybe we can clear this up."

The bank officer looked like she might faint.

"This," I said, "is my great-grandfather, Maurice. He opened the account with your bank many years ago when he was still a person."

The bank officer leaned heavily against the counter so she wouldn't fall down.

"This individual does, indeed, appear to be...a cat," she whispered.

"You're darned tootin' I am," said Great-Grandpa Maurice. "And if you don't mind, I'd like to withdraw all the money in my account and give it to my family."

"Are you able to...sign for it?" she whispered, barely able to speak.

"Hey, dollface," he said, "I'm a cat. Maybe you noticed. I don't happen to have an opposable thumb. So I can't hold a pen."

"If you're unable to sign," she whispered, "we would be unable to...give you the money."

"Why the heck not?" he asked.

"It would not be...consistent with company policy," she whispered, her eyes now squeezed shut.

"Then how's about changing company policy?" he said. "From now on, anytime somebody gets reincarnated as a cat and comes in to get his money, all he has to do is ask for it. What do you say?"

The bank officer took a deep breath.

"I just don't...know if we can do that," she said.

"OK then, get me Morty," said Great-Grandpa Maurice.

"Who's Morty?" asked the bank officer.

"Who's Morty?" repeated Great-Grandpa Maurice. "You mean to say you don't know Morton F. Acropolis, the founder of the bank?"

And with that, the cat leapt off the

counter and hotfooted it down the hall.

"Now just a minute there," the bank officer called after him. "I can't let you— "

Great-Grandpa Maurice stopped in front of a fancy door. It said "Morton F. Acropolis" on the front.

"Hey, Morty!" yelled Great-Grandpa Maurice. "You in there?"

"Maurice?" called a surprised voice from inside the office. "Maurice, is that you?"

The cat pushed the founder's door open with his nose and walked inside. My dad, Grandma Leah, and I followed close behind. The bank officer came right after us.

Behind a long desk that looked like some kind of antique sat the oldest man I had ever seen. He was also one of the shortest.

I doubt if he was a lot taller than me, and he had on a pair of glasses with amazingly thick lenses.

"Hey, Morty, great to see you!" said the cat.

"Maurice, you old dog, is that you?" cried Mr. Acropolis. He squinted through his glasses and peered over the top of his desk. "My eyes aren't what they used to be. But I'd recognize that voice anywhere, even after all these years!"

"So how have you been, Morty?"

"Never mind me, what about you, Maurice? I heard you were dead."

"I was," said the cat. "But I'm better now. Listen, Morty, I got a problem. Maybe you can help me."

"For you, Maurice? Anything. What can I do?"

"Sir," said the bank officer, "do you realize you're talking to a c—"

"Quiet, Lola," snapped the old man. "I haven't seen this man in ages."

"But he's not a man, sir," said the bank officer, "he's a c—"

"Quiet!" shouted Mr. Acropolis. "Go ahead, Maurice, what can I do for you?"

"It's the money I made on the hot dog sweater, Morty. I'd like to withdraw it from my account. But this young lady here tells me I can't."

"Poppycock!" roared Mr. Acropolis. "I invested in that hot dog sweater myself. Smartest move I ever made. Give the man his money, Lola!"

"But, Mr. Acropolis, he's unable to sign for it."

"Why's that?"

"He can't hold a pen in his paws," she said.

"Well, I can't hold a pen in *my* paws either," said Mr. Acropolis. "A man gets to be our age, dear, there are certain things he can't do by himself any longer. Help him, for the love of Pete!"

"Y-yes, sir," said the bank officer.

And so we all walked out of Mr. Acropolis's office. Then, with shaking hands, the bank officer put a pen between the cat's paws and helped him sign his name. Then she wrote out a check and handed it to us. My dad looked at the amount and whistled.

"Maurice, I thought you said there was thirty thousand dollars in this account," he said.

"How much is in there?" asked Maurice.

"Closer to ninety," said my dad.

"Ninety thousand dollars?" asked Grandma Leah. It was the first thing she'd said since we'd arrived at the bank.

"Well, that's after more than thirty years of interest," said my dad.

"And you really want us to have this?" I asked.

"On one condition," said Maurice.

"What's that?"

"That you leave me enough for a first-class, one-way ticket to Palm Beach, and a few years' rent in a deluxe pet hotel, with a standing order for herring and sour cream every morning, and a glass of schnapps every night."

"You're not going to live with us?" I said.

"As much as I love you, Zack," said Maurice, "I've always wanted to spend my golden years in Florida. I understand there are folks down there who might be willing to invest a few dollars in inventions of a somewhat speculative nature."

~⌐~

So Maurice went off to live the good life in Florida. But before he did he had the bank officer open his safe-deposit box. There it was. A baseball signed by Lou Gehrig, Ty Cobb, and Rogers Hornsby.

"This is for you, kid," he said to me. "I was going to keep it, but hey, what the heck does an old pussycat need with an old baseball anyway?"

Even though Great-Grandpa Maurice was kind of pushy, I was really sad to see him go.

"Hey, Zack," he said, "cheer up. Now you can go back to the animal shelter and get that little tuxedo kitten you were look-ing at."

"But you said he has fleas and worms and never learned how to use a litter box," I replied.

"Maybe so," he said. "But there's one thing about him that might make you over-look all that."

"What?"

"In a former life he was Babe Ruth."

What else happens to Zack?

Find out in

ZAP! I'm a

Mind Reader

Lightning must have knocked out the power. I was pretty freaked out, alone in the dark science room.

Carefully I got up from my desk. From the flashes of lightning, I could almost see well enough to get to the door.

When I was about halfway there, I got this really creepy feeling. The feeling that I wasn't alone in the room. And right after that, I picked up a thought. It said, *There he is! Now I have him! The time to kill is now!*

THE ZACK FILES™

OUT-OF-THIS-WORLD FAN CLUB!

Looking for even more info on all the strange, otherworldly happenings going on in *The Zack Files*? Get the inside scoop by becoming a member of *The Zack Files* Out-Of-This-World Fan Club! Just send in the form below and we'll send you your *Zack Files* Out-Of-This-World Fan Club kit including an official fan club membership card, a really cool *Zack Files* magnet, and a newsletter featuring excerpts from Zack's upcoming paranormal adventures, supernatural news from around the world, puzzles, and more! And as a member you'll continue to receive the newsletter six times a year! The best part is—it's all free!

✂ ---

☐ Yes! I want to check out *The Zack Files*
   Out-Of-This-World Fan Club!

name: _____ age: _____

address: _____

city/town: _____ state: ____ zip: _____

Send this form to: Penguin Putnam Books for
                             Young Readers
                             Mass Merchandise Marketing
                             Dept. ZACK
                             345 Hudson Street
                             New York, NY 10014

What else happens to Zack?
Find out in
A Ghost Named Wanda

That's when we heard a very loud noise. A big bag of peanut M&Ms that was on a shelf just kind of exploded. All the M&Ms flew upward. They hit the ceiling, and stuck there. The way they stuck spelled out a message. It said:

OK OK HERE I AM WHAT NOW

"Oh, my gosh," I said softly.

"Oh, my gosh," said my dad.

I couldn't believe it—I had made contact with an actual evil spirit, with an actual spirit of a dead person.

THE ZACK FILES™

Through the Medicine Cabinet

For Judith, and for the real Zack,
with love—D.G.

THE ZACK FILES™

Through the Medicine Cabinet

By Dan Greenburg

Illustrated by Jack E. Davis

GROSSET & DUNLAP • NEW YORK

I'd like to thank my editors,
Jane O'Connor and Judy Donnelly,
who make the process of writing and revising
so much fun, and without whom
these books would not exist.

I also want to thank
Jennifer Dussling and Laura Driscoll
for their terrific ideas.

Text copyright © 1996 by Dan Greenburg. Illustrations copyright © 1996 by Jack E. Davis. All rights reserved. Published by Grosset & Dunlap, a division of Penguin Putnam Books for Young Readers, New York. THE ZACK FILES is a trademark of The Putnam & Grosset Group. GROSSET & DUNLAP is a trademark of Grosset & Dunlap, Inc. Published simultaneously in Canada. Printed in the U.S.A.

Library of Congress Cataloging-in-Publication Data

Greenburg, Dan.
  Through the medicine cabinet / by Dan Greenburg ; illustrated by Jack E. Davis.
    p.   cm. — (The Zack files)
    Summary: After Zack opens his medicine cabinet one morning and sees a boy who could be his double staring back at him, he enters a parallel universe.
    [1. Supernatural—Fiction.]   I. Davis, Jack E., ill. II. Title. III. Series: Greenburg, Dan.   Zack files.
PZ7.G8278Th 1996
[Fic]—dc20   96-7107
                                                                                  CIP
                                                                                   AC

ISBN   0-448-41262-4   F G H I J

Chapter 1

I'm what you'd call a pretty normal kid.
My name is Zack, which is a pretty normal
name. I'm ten years old, which is a pretty
normal age. I have normal brown hair and
eyes. I have slightly crooked teeth, which is
normal at my age. And I live in a big apartment building in New York. I always
thought my building was normal, at least
until the thing I'm about to tell you
happened.

I've got to admit I've always been interested in weird stuff. Stuff like dead people crawling out of their graves at night. Or guys who stare at you and then suddenly their heads explode. I haven't actually seen those things. But who am I to say they couldn't happen?

Anyway, the time I want to tell you about happened at the beginning of spring vacation. My dad arranged to take me down to Florida. We were going to visit the New York Yankees at their spring training camp.

My parents are divorced. Part of the time I live with my dad. He's a writer, and he gets to do lots of cool things. Like go to spring training and then write about it in a magazine. I can't believe he gets paid to do this stuff. Neither can he.

Saturday morning was when we were planning to leave. I was so excited, I woke up at about 6:00 A.M. The minute I opened my eyes, I realized something. I had forgotten to put my retainer in my mouth before I went to sleep. Where the heck was it?

A retainer, in case you don't know, is braces that you wear on your teeth at night. I don't exactly love my retainer. It's made of wire and pink plastic. It's really gross-looking, especially when you take it out and put it on the table at lunch.

My dad hates when I lose my retainer. They cost twelve hundred dollars, I think. Or a hundred and twelve. I forget which.

I left one retainer in a pair of jeans, which went in the laundry. It melted to the inside of the pocket. One got chewed up in

my Grandma Leah's garbage disposal. Another got flushed down the toilet. Another one I'm almost positive a robber stole while I was out of my room, although I've never been able to prove this.

All in all, I have not lost more than seven of them. Eight, tops.

I was sure my retainer was in the medicine cabinet in the bathroom, instead of in my mouth, where it should have been. I got up and opened the door of the medicine cabinet. Yes! There was my retainer. But then, just as I was about to close the cabinet door, something weird happened. Something very weird. The back of the medicine cabinet opened. And there, staring right in my face, was a boy who looked almost exactly like me!

Chapter 2

A boy who looked just like me? How could that be? I was so startled, I knocked over my retainer. It fell into his bathroom. Then we both screamed and slammed our medicine cabinet doors shut.

What the heck was happening here?

Very slowly I opened the medicine cabinet again. Nope. There was nobody on the other side. I pushed against the back of it. It didn't open. Very weird.

So where was my retainer? I figured I'd better check out the apartment next door. An old lady named Mrs. Taradash lives there.

Mrs. Taradash is kind of cranky. I know she isn't too happy about the basketball hoop I have mounted on my wall. She's complained to my dad lots of times. When I slam-dunk, she says it's like a 5.7 tremor on the Richter scale.

But maybe Mrs. Taradash had a grand-son. Maybe her grandson looked almost exactly like me. And maybe her medicine cabinet was hooked up to ours on the other side.

I knew this explanation didn't make much sense. But it was all I could come up with.

I got dressed. Then I slipped quietly out

of our apartment. I knocked on Mrs. Taradash's door. There was no answer. I knocked again. It took a while before somebody opened it. Mrs. Taradash was in a fuzzy robe and fuzzy slippers. Her hair was all messed up. And she was rubbing her eyes. She didn't seem all that thrilled to see me, if you want to know the truth.

"I'm sorry to bother you, Mrs. Taradash," I said. "I was wondering whether I could get my retainer out of your bathroom."

"Your what, precious?" she said.

She calls all kids "precious." But you can tell she doesn't think they are.

"My retainer," I said.

"What in the name of heaven is that, precious?"

"A retainer is braces made out of wire

~ 8 ~

and pink plastic, which sometimes falls down disposals or toilets," I explained. "Mine fell into your apartment when your grandson opened the medicine cabinet door."

Mrs. Taradash looked at me like I was cuckoo.

"I don't have a grandson, precious," she said.

"You don't have a grandson? Then who opened the other side of my medicine cabinet just now?"

The bottom half of her face smiled. But the top half was frowning. It looked like both halves were fighting with each other. She tried to close the door on my foot.

"Please don't close the door, Mrs. Taradash," I begged her. "I lost my retainer in your apartment. It's the eighth one

that's gotten away from me. Maybe the ninth. If I don't get it back, my dad will kill me. You wouldn't want that on your conscience, would you?"

She opened the door and looked at me.

"What do you want?" she said. It was more hissing than talking. And she seemed to have forgotten the word "precious."

"Just my retainer," I said, "which the boy who's not your grandson will tell you fell into your bathroom from my medicine cabinet. Please just let me look for it."

"If I let you look," she said, "will you go away and let me get back to sleep?"

"Yes, ma'am," I said.

She sighed a deep sigh. Then she waved me into the apartment.

I went in.

Weird. Everywhere you looked, there were stuffed animals. And I don't mean cuddly teddy bears, either. I mean real dead animals that were stuffed by a taxidermist. Squirrels, rabbits, beavers, chipmunks. They were all frozen in weird poses. And they stared at you through their beady glass eyes. They really gave me the creeps.

I hurried into the bathroom and looked around. There was no retainer on the floor or anywhere else. I opened the medicine cabinet. I pushed against the back. It didn't budge. So I closed the medicine cabinet door.

"Satisfied?" she hissed.

I had a sudden feeling that if I didn't

leave, her eyes would start glowing red. Then she'd grab me and try to stuff me. There I'd be, standing alongside the other animals in a weird frozen pose, staring at visitors through beady glass eyes.

I apologized and hotfooted it back to my dad's apartment. I didn't have a clue what had happened. I began to think I'd dreamed the whole thing. But if I did, then where was my retainer?

On the way back to my bedroom, I passed my bathroom. Out of the corner of my eye I thought I saw something.

My medicine cabinet door.

It was slowly creeping open.

Chapter 3

I raced into my bathroom. I yanked open the door of the medicine cabinet all the way.

There he was! The same boy I'd seen before.

"Hey!" I said.

He didn't slam the door this time. I think he was too stunned. He kept staring. I was staring too. He really did look a whole lot

like me. Only his teeth were a lot more crooked.

"Who are you?" I asked.

"Zeke," he said.

"I'm Zack."

"I know."

"You don't live next door," I said. "Do you?"

He shook his head.

"Then where do you live?"

"Someplace else. Someplace nearby, but kind of far away, too. Someplace you might think is weird."

"You live in New Jersey?"

He shook his head.

"Then where?"

"Have you ever heard of Newer York?" he said.

"Is that up near Poughkeepsie?" I asked.

He sighed and rolled his eyes like I had just said the stupidest thing in the world. I had a sudden thought.

"Hey," I said, "is this something really weird that I'm going to be sorry I got myself involved in?"

"I have time for just one more question," he said. "And then I have to go."

"OK," I said. "Do you have my retainer? I think it fell on your side."

He suddenly tried to slam the door. But I was too fast for him. I stuck my arm into the medicine cabinet. That stopped him from shutting it. He grabbed my hand and tried to pry it off the door. I grabbed his wrist.

"Let go!" he shouted.

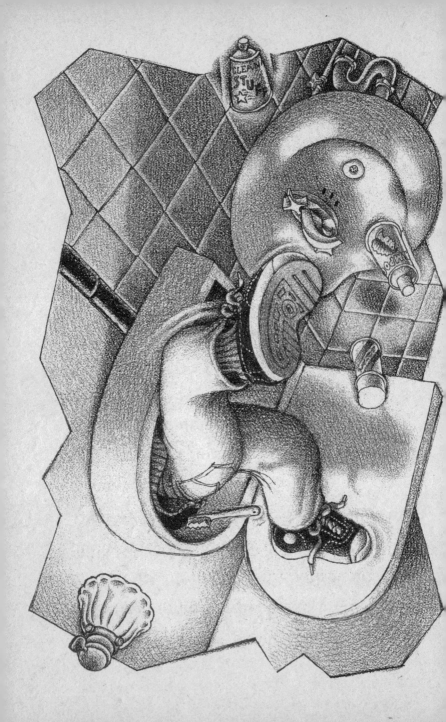

"Not till you give me my retainer!"

He tried to pull away. I held on tight. He backed up. I hung on with both hands. He pulled me through the medicine cabinet. Then we both fell onto the floor in his bathroom.

"Now you've done it!" he shouted. "Now you've really done it!" He looked frightened.

"Done what?" I asked.

"The one thing nobody is ever supposed to do," he said.

"What's that?" I asked.

"Cross over into a parallel universe!"

Chapter 4

"What the heck is a parallel universe?" I asked.

Zeke looked around nervously.

"Shhhh!" he shouted. "Somebody might hear you!"

"You're the one who's shouting," I said. "What the heck is a parallel universe?"

"Well, it's kind of like this," said Zeke. "Our universe is right next to yours. It's so

close you wouldn't believe it. It even takes up some of the same space as yours. Only you can't usually see us. Except on Opening Days. Like today."

"Today isn't Opening Day," I said. "The baseball season doesn't start for a couple months yet."

Zeke sighed and shook his head.

"The kind of Opening Day I'm talking about," he said, "has nothing to do with baseball. It's when your universe and mine move right next to each other. It doesn't happen a lot. It'll be years before it happens again."

"Sort of like an eclipse?" I asked.

"Sort of," he said. "When it's Opening Day, we can look through certain openings, like a medicine cabinet. Then we

can see your universe. Which, by the way, isn't any better than ours."

"I didn't say it was better," I said. "Did I say it was better?"

"Maybe not. But I bet that's what you were thinking," he said. "We've got everything you've got. And it's just as good, believe me. Maybe even better."

"OK, OK!" I said. Then I picked myself up off the floor. I got my first good look at the parallel universe in Zeke's bathroom.

Hmmmm.

It looked pretty much the same as mine. Only different. First of all, there was something odd about the sink. There were two faucets. But they were marked Cold and Not So Cold.

Then I looked at the roll of toilet paper by

the toilet. It looked like sandpaper. I hoped I wouldn't be in the parallel universe long enough to have to use the bathroom.

I noticed there was a lot of water on the floor. When I glanced at the shower I saw why. Instead of a shower curtain, there were venetian blinds.

"So what's Newer York like?" I asked.

"Outstanding," he said.

"How many channels do you get on TV?" I asked.

He looked at me suspiciously.

"You get more than one channel?" he asked.

"Never mind," I said.

"Hey," he said. "Everything in the Big Banana is as good as anything you've got in New York."

"Oh, you call Newer York the Big Banana," I said. "Like we call New York the Big Apple."

"Bananas are a lot cooler fruit than apples," he said.

"Look," I said, "I'm sure everything in your universe is every bit as cool as ours, OK? Now can I have my retainer? And then will you please help me cross back over?"

"Zeke, are you packing?" The voice sounded a lot like my dad's.

"Yeah, Dad!" Zeke called back.

"Well, hurry up! The cab is coming at 8:00."

I looked at Zeke strangely.

"You're going somewhere with your dad?" I asked.

"Yeah. We have to catch a plane."

I got a sudden dizzy feeling.

"Your dad isn't by any chance taking you to the training camp of the New York Yankees, is he?" I asked.

"No."

"Well, *that's* a relief," I said.

"He's taking me to the training camp of the Newer York Yunkees. They're a triple-A minor league team. But they're just as good as the Yankees."

"Oh my gosh," I said softly. "Your life is just the same as mine, except a little different, isn't it?"

"Well, duh!" he said. "That's what a parallel universe is, Zack." He sounded like he was talking to a fourth-grader. I didn't appreciate that, since I happen to be

in the fifth grade. "You want to know the truth? I'm a little tired of living in the one that's the copy and not the one that's the original."

"You are? But you just said—"

"Never mind what I said. I may live in a parallel universe. But I'm not stupid. Don't you think I'd rather be going to see the Yankees train than the Yunkees?"

"I can't hear you, Zeke!" called his dad. "Are you talking to me?"

"No, to myself!" he shouted. Then to me he said, "Hey, I've got an idea. Why don't we switch places? I'll go to the Yankees' training camp with your dad. You can go to the Yunkees' with mine."

"No way," I said.

"Never mind," he said. "I didn't want to do it anyway."

"Have you packed your retainer yet?" called Zeke's dad.

"Don't worry about it!" Zeke answered nervously.

"Oh my God," I said. "Don't tell me you can't find your retainer either!"

"So what?" he said.

This was freaking me out.

"Zeke," called his dad. He sounded like he was right outside the door. "Are you in there?"

Zeke looked scared.

"We can't let him see you here," he whispered. "You've got to hide!"

"Where?"

"Here."

He led me to the bathtub. He pulled back the blinds and pushed me inside. Then I heard him open and close the medicine

cabinet door. And then nothing. What was
he up to?

I looked at my watch. I had only a half
hour before our cab came. What was I
doing hiding in a bathtub in a parallel universe? And how was I ever going to get
back to mine?

I peeked through the blind. Zeke was
nowhere in sight. And then I knew.

That little rat had sneaked back through
the medicine cabinet door into my
universe!

Chapter 5

I was in a panic.

At this very minute, Zeke was pretending to be me. He was getting ready to leave with my dad for the Yankee training camp in Florida!

I heard a knock at the bathroom door.

"Zeke, did you hear me? Are you ready?" said his father's voice.

I held my breath.

The door opened. Zeke's father came into the bathroom. Just then I sneezed.

"Achooooo!"

"Zeke? Are you in the shower?"

"No, sir," I said.

The blinds were pulled up. There stood a dad who looked almost exactly like mine.

At first I was scared he might be mad. But then he began to laugh.

"What are you doing in the shower with your clothes on?" he asked.

"Resting," I said.

"There's no time for resting, Zeke. Our cab is coming in about half an hour. Have you got your retainer? Are you all packed?"

"Pretty much," I said.

He looked at me oddly and frowned.

"You look a little different, son. Did you

comb your hair a new way this morning?"

"Yes, sir. I did. That's exactly what I did."

"Uh huh. OK. Well, I still have a few things to do. Zeke, could you run to the dry cleaners quickly and pick up all our cleaning?"

The cleaners! The only place I wanted to go was back through the medicine cabinet. But what could I say?

"Uh, s-sure," I stammered. "What cleaners would that be again?"

"You know. The one across the street and down the block."

"Uh huh. And what block would that be again?"

He looked at me and raised an eyebrow.

"C'mon," he said. "You've gone there

lots of times. Just get going. We have to leave soon."

"OK," I said.

He handed me a receipt and a twenty-dollar bill. Then he walked out of the bath-room.

The twenty-dollar bill looked strange. It was enormous. And when I examined it closely, I saw that along the top it said "The Untied States of America." The picture on all the twenty-dollar bills I've seen is of Andrew Jackson. This one was of somebody with bushy hair, a beard, and nose-glasses. His name was Slappy Kupperman.

I left the apartment and went down in the elevator. Then I got outside. I wanted to get to the cleaners and back as fast as I could.

At the corner I waited for traffic to stop. It was taking forever. Then I looked up at the traffic signal and I saw why. Instead of a red and a green light, there were four lights.

The lights said, "STOP," "NOT YET," "HOLD ON," and "OK, GO ALREADY."

Newer York sure was a weird place.

A big billboard to my right said, "WE LOVE NEWER YORK! JUST AS GOOD AS NEW YORK. MAYBE BETTER!" Well, I didn't think so. I wanted to get back to my own universe.

I did manage to find the cleaners. I got Zeke's dad's clothes. Then I beat it out of there. I went back down the block. But I must have gotten messed up somehow. Because when I got to the corner, the big

billboard should have been to my left. But it wasn't there at all.

I took a quick look around. Nothing looked familiar. Then I saw a big apartment building across the street. It had a fancy canopy. It looked a whole lot like one in my own neighborhood in my own universe. The Beekman Arms Plaza Apartments. I thought maybe the doorman could help me find my way back to Zeke's. The problem was, I didn't even know Zeke's stupid address. All I knew was that it would probably be like mine. Only a little different.

I ran to the building. But there wasn't any doorman. In fact, there wasn't even any building! What I thought was a building was only a fake front, like a movie set.

The bushes in front of it were made of green plastic. There was a tag on them. It said, "Realistic bushes. Last longer. Need less care. Better than real."

I gulped. I felt like I was in a dream. One of those really awful ones where, no matter how hard you try to get someplace, you can't, and then you puke.

In the middle of the street I saw an open manhole. There were police barricades around it. Signs said, "DANGER ON OPENING DAYS! FALLING IN WOULD BE STUPID! ALSO PAINFUL! DID WE MENTION ILLEGAL?"

Hey! This could be another way to get back to my universe! If I couldn't find my way back to Zeke's and go through the medicine cabinet, maybe I could climb

through here. Going through the sewers would be pretty gross, of course. But I didn't care. At least I'd come out on the right side.

I waited for the traffic light to change. Again it took forever. Then I raced up to the manhole. Now was the time to make my move. But just as I stooped down, I felt a heavy hand on my shoulder.

I looked up. A big policeman was standing over me. He seemed kind of scary. But then I looked at the gun in his holster. It was a Super Soaker.

"You wouldn't want to get too close and fall into New York," he said. "Now would you, sonny?"

"Oh boy, sir. I sure wouldn't want to do that," I said.

We both laughed pretty hard at the idea I'd want to do anything as stupid as fall into New York.

"Well then, step away from there," he said.

I did. He stayed right next to the manhole. I don't think he trusted me. But with his Super Soaker he didn't seem so scary anymore. I decided to ask his help.

"Um, Officer," I said, "I'm kind of lost. I was on my way home. But I must have taken a wrong turn or something."

"What's your address, son?" he asked.

"My address?"

"Yes."

"Uh, well, I'm not exactly sure," I said. "I mean it seems to have temporarily slipped my mind."

"Your address has slipped your mind?"

"Temporarily."

He looked at me strangely. But he listened while I described Zeke's building.

"Oh, I know the one you mean," he said. "I'll take you there."

He took me by the hand. Then he led me down the block and around the corner.

There it was, Zeke's building! I thanked him all over the place, and then I took off. He was probably glad to get rid of me.

Right in front of Zeke's building was a newsstand. It was just like the one in front of my own building. On the front page of all the newspapers were big headlines:

"DANGER! OPENING DAY ARRIVES! CITIZENS WARNED NOT TO TAKE CHANCES!"

Danger? What danger? I picked up a paper and started to read.

"Today, in the early hours of the morning, citizens of Newer York will once again be able to peek through any of several openings and actually observe life in our sister universe. 'Do not attempt to cross over into the alternate universe!' warns Professor Roland Fenster at the Newer York Institute of Parallel Universes. 'The openings should appear somewhere in the vicinity of 6:00 A.M. They will then shut down tight again approximately two hours later. Once shut, they will not reopen for as many as thirty years. Thirty years would be one heck of a long time to spend in a universe that's rumored to be better than ours, but isn't.'"

I looked at my watch. Yikes! It was 7:45 A.M. I had just fifteen minutes before the cab came and Zeke left for Florida with my dad. And before the doors to my universe slammed shut for thirty years!

I raced into Zeke's building.

Chapter

6

I arrived back in Zeke's apartment out of breath. I dropped Zeke's dad's cleaning in the hallway. I raced into the bathroom.

I pushed hard against the back of the medicine cabinet. But I couldn't make the darned thing budge. Zeke obviously knew more about traveling between universes than I did!

And then I heard somebody behind me. I

whirled around to find Zeke's dad looking at me strangely.

"Zeke," he said, "what are you doing?"

Should I tell him the truth? Could I trust him? Or was he the enemy? I didn't know. But time was running out. And I didn't see that I had much choice.

"Listen, sir," I said, "this is going to sound sort of incredible. But it's the truth, so help me."

"All right, Zeke," he said. "But make it fast. We have less than fifteen minutes before the cab comes."

"OK," I said. "First of all, I'm not your son, Zeke. I'm somebody else who looks just like him. And my name is Zack. I live in the parallel universe. My dad and I were getting ready to go to the Yankees' training

camp. Just like you and Zeke were getting ready to go to the Yunkees' training camp. Only I dropped my retainer through the medicine cabinet. I lost it, the same as Zeke lost his."

Zeke's dad's mouth dropped open. He smacked his forehead with his hand.

"I can't be-lieve it!" he said.

"It's true, though, sir," I said. "I swear."

"Zeke has lost his retainer?" he said in a dazed voice. "That's the tenth one so far this year."

Wow! Zeke was even worse than me!

"Do you know how much those things cost?" he asked.

"Either twelve hundred dollars or a hundred and twelve dollars," I said quickly. "But didn't you hear the other stuff I told you?"

"Yes, yes, yes. Of course I did," he said. "Your name is Zack. You live in the parallel universe on the other side of the medicine cabinet, blah, blah, blah."

"You don't believe me, do you?" I said.

"Why shouldn't I believe you?" he said. "Everybody in Newer York knows about your universe. It's not like it's a big secret or anything. And it isn't any better than ours either, by the way."

Boy, this was a touchy subject with these guys!

"I never said it was better," I said. "Look, sir, you seem to know a lot about parallel universes. So maybe you know how to slip back through the medicine cabinet to mine. Like Zeke did just now."

"Zeke?" he said. "He crossed over?"

I nodded. I really had Zeke's dad's attention now.

"But it's almost 7:50!" Zeke's dad smacked his forehead again. "At 8:00 Opening Day will shut down completely!"

"My point exactly, sir," I said. "I'd be miserable if that happened. Not that I wouldn't love living here, I mean. Because I think it's at least as good as my universe. And maybe even better. But the thing is, I'd really miss my mom and dad."

"OK, OK," said Zeke's dad. "This is what you have to do. Put your hand on the back wall of the medicine cabinet."

I did.

"Close your eyes. Take a deep breath. Now visualize the back wall opening. Let me know if you feel anything."

I did everything he said. It started to work. The wall was starting to feel kind of springy. I opened my eyes in time to see it sort of melt away.

Chapter 7

"Hi, Zack," said a familiar face.

"Zeke!" said Zeke's dad. "Oh, thank heavens!"

"Zeke!" I said. "Were you coming back?"

He looked embarrassed.

"I got homesick," he said. "I mean, your dad is awfully nice, Zack. He really is. But he's not my dad. And this isn't my

universe. I figured you must feel the same way. Even though Newer York is just as cool as New York."

My dad appeared on the other side of the medicine cabinet.

"Dad!" I said.

"Hi, Zack," said my dad. Then he turned to Zeke's dad. "Hi, Don," he said. "Long time, no see."

"Hi, Dan," said Zeke's dad to my dad.

They shook hands through the medicine cabinet.

"You two *know* each other?" I asked, amazed.

"Yeah, we met when we were your age," said Zeke's dad. "But it wasn't through a medicine cabinet. It was through a dryer in the laundromat."

"Yeah," said my dad. "I always wondered what happened to odd socks that got lost in the laundry. Who'd have guessed they go to the parallel universe?"

"That was quite an Opening Day," said Zeke's dad. "Not much laundry got dried. But we sure had fun. Your dad thought I lived in the dryer."

Both my dad and Zeke's dad started laughing their heads off.

"Uh, excuse me for interrupting," I said. "This is all very interesting. But it's now 7:55."

"Oh, right, right!" said Zeke's dad. He looked through the cabinet at Zeke. "Do you still want to go to the Yunkees' training camp, son?"

"I sure do!" said Zeke.

"Then let me pull you through," said Zeke's dad.

So Zeke crawled back into his own universe. I crawled back into mine.

"I'm sorry, Zack," said Zeke. "I was a real jerk."

"You were," I said. "But I forgive you."

Cab horns were now honking on both sides of the cabinet.

"Well, so long, guys," I said.

"See you again sometime," said Zeke.

"Maybe at the next Opening Day," I said.

"OK," said Zeke.

He fished something out of his pocket. He handed it to me through the cabinet. It was my retainer!

"You swiped my retainer?" I said.

He nodded sheepishly.

"But I couldn't keep it," he said.

"Because you knew it was wrong."

"Yeah," he said. "Also, it didn't fit."

Then all of a sudden, the grandfather clock in our hallway started chiming.

It was 8:00.

We waved good-bye to each other. Then, instead of facing Zeke and his dad, I was looking at shelves with toothpaste and deodorant. I pushed hard against the back wall of the medicine cabinet. I visualized like crazy. But nothing happened.

So that's how I discovered the parallel universe. And every time I open my medicine cabinet, I think of Zeke and his dad. I kind of miss them. It's funny to think that they're so close, and yet so far away.

The next time I see Zeke, I could have a

son of my own. Weird! I wonder what he'll be like. Hey, wouldn't it be cool if he's just like me? In every way except one: I hope he doesn't ever need to wear a retainer!

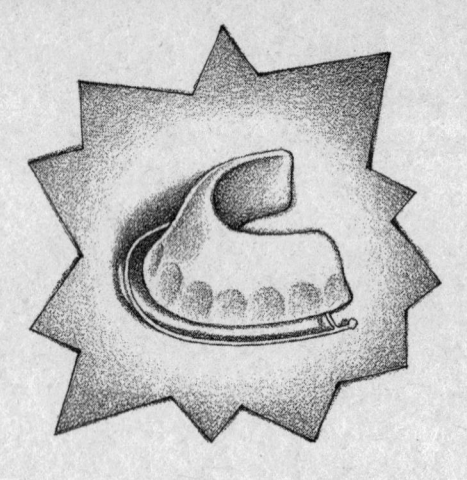